HAUNTINGS & HAVOC

Written by Stacey Rourke

Chapter One

Gravel crunched under the wheels of the battered, short-bodied pick-up truck. Slowing to a stop, the woods surrounding it seemed to hold its breath in nervous anticipation. Rain pelted the windows, the wipers squeaking from side to side. The sprawling darkness was illuminated only by the truck's headlights. On a hill in the distance sat the Crane's Roost Inn. The once regal structure was now reduced to an abandoned crypt of loss and decay. The grass was overgrown. The windows boarded. Cracks could be seen in the walls and foundation. The only thing more foreboding than the structure itself was the legacy of the family who created it.

That was enough to send shivers down the spine and quicken the breath.

"You know, there's a cliff at the beach where you can park and look out at the ocean." Casey twirled a lock of blonde hair around her index finger and batted her sapphire eyes in her boyfriend's direction. "Not that I don't appreciate the spooky ambiance of an old hotel, but the scenery at the beach would be way better."

Putting the truck in park, Steve clicked off his headlights and stretched his arm across the bench seat behind her. With the tips of his fingers, he traced along her shoulder blades. "First of all, there is no prettier scenery than you…"

"Well played," she said with a coquettish giggle.

"Secondly," scooting closer, he dipped his head to let his hot breath tease over her neck, "the beach is a very public location, and what I want to do with you is very, very private."

Closing her eyes, Casey treated herself to the blissful taste of his salty-sweet lips. "So, what you're saying is that you brought me out here with the solitary goal of getting laid?" she murmured with her mouth pressed to his.

Steve's breath caught, his voice throaty with desire. "Saying it was my goal makes it sound carefully planned and plotted. I prefer to think of it as hopeful expectation. Like a kid on Christmas about to unwrap," he made the bold move to cup the rise of her breast in his palm, "the best present ever."

Fueled by teenage hormones, the two met in a rush of frantic passion. Hitched breaths. Hands wandering. Inhibitions and modesty all but forgotten.

Steve was fumbling with the zipper of his pants, in hopes of coercing her—at the very least—into an awkward hand job, when Casey bristled.

"D-did you hear that?"

"Did I yell yippee out loud?" Steve didn't stop peppering her neck and shoulder with kisses. "I thought I was just thinking it."

Lips red from their aggressive foreplay, Casey playfully pushed her beau away. "I'm serious. It sounded like heavy footsteps crunching in the grass."

Pulling back, Steve fought off a scowl at the thought of this being yet another distraction meant to preserve her angelic virginity. They had dated for six months, and the only love he'd had was from his own hand. How patient was a guy expected to be?

Unable to hide his annoyance, he let his head fall back against the seat. "The place has been abandoned for years, Cas. That's why I picked it. But if you want to go, we'll go."

Eyes wide and scanning the darkness, Casey held up one hand to silence him. "I'm not kidding!" she hissed. "Shut up and listen."

Noting the flare of her nostrils and firm set of her jaw, Steve relented simply to appease her. Lifting his head, he pantomimed zipping his lips, and listened.

Sticks snapped.

Leaves crunched.

Something was moving their way fast.

"Shit, what is that?" Steve asked the darkness.

The pair stared out into the night, searching all sides for signs of something, anything, moving.

They saw nothing beyond the rain, yet that did little to calm their nerves.

"You heard that, right?" Casey's voice boiled with barely contained panic.

"I did. Where was it coming from?"

Casey glanced toward the abandoned hotel in the same instant lightning lit up the sky. What she saw lurking there made a fist of terror tighten around her throat. "Oh, God. Steve! Up by the hotel! Look! There's someone on the hill watching us!"

Lightning flashed again and the pair screamed. The figure by the entrance had moved to stand mere feet from the truck, having crossed that great distance in nothing more than a blink.

"Aw, fuck no," Steve mumbled more to himself than to his date. Sitting up straight, he threw the truck into drive. His tires spun on the wet dirt yet couldn't catch enough traction to move.

Casey swiveled in her seat, her eyes wide and unblinking. "What's happening? Why aren't we moving? Steve, I want to go!"

"No shit! So do I!" Once more he hammered his foot down on the accelerator, accomplishing nothing more than flinging mud along the wheel wells.

Another flash and the figure stood at the hood of the truck, looming over them in a heavy wool hood that obscured its face from view. The glimpse was momentary, then they were plunged into inky darkness once more.

"Who is that?" Casey's hand shot out, clutching Steve's sleeve in a white knuckled grip. "Where did they go?"

"I don't fucking know!" Steve's scream matched hers with frantic intensity. With a flick of his wrist, he turned on the headlights.

There was nothing there. The shadowy figure had vanished without a trace. Knowing whoever it was lurked out there somewhere caused both their hearts to hammer against their ribs. Pulses pounding in their temples, they sat in silence and waited... for what, they couldn't say.

The rain slowed to a drizzle.

While the storm was blowing over, their fear was not.

"Is... is it gone?" Casey stammered.

Leaning forward, Steve squinted to see beyond his headlights. "I don't know. If it is, I need to get out and put something under the back tires. That's the only way we'll get enough traction to get out of here."

"No!" Casey's grip on his shirt tightened. "Haven't you watched, like, any scary movie *ever*? If you go out there, you're dead! We both are."

Before Steve could answer, the roof of the truck caved under a heavy weight. At Casey's blood-curdling scream, Steve gathered her protectively in his arms. Their stares were locked skyward as the metal overhead creaked and groaned.

In stillness they waited.

Breath held.

Fingers laced tight.

They waited a beat... then another.

"Fuck this," Steve grumbled under his breath. "We're not going to stay here and be tormented by some freak. On the count of three, we're going to throw our doors open and run. Do you hear me? Meet me at the tailgate, grab my hand, and we're going to run like hell back towards the road. Do you understand?"

Unable to form words between her choked sobs, Casey shook her head. "No. No, I can't..."

"Yes, you can." Raising their linked fingers to his lips, he dotted a kiss between her knuckles. "And you will. On the count of three. Okay?"

"Please don't make me do this..."

"One..."

"Oh, God, no. Steve, I can't."

"Two..."

Suddenly, black hands with talon-like nails burst through the backs of their seats, seizing them by the shoulders and pinning them where they sat.

"*Three.*" A devilish rasp rattled the windows, making their flesh prickle with the powerful presence of an entity not to be ignored.

Wriggling free, the pair flung open the doors and spilled out onto the muddy earth. Ground squishing beneath their feet, they scrambled to reconnect in the glow of the brake lights.

A chivalrous nature Steve didn't know himself possible of took over as he cradled Casey's head against his chest and braced himself to face off with whatever beastie lurked at the desolate inn. "*Who are you? What do you want?*"

Still on the roof, the shadowy being shrugged off the hood of their cloak. Or, more aptly, *my* cloak. It was in that moment I revealed myself; an enchanting beauty molded into art by the scars that marred one side of my face. Burned, boiled, and left to rot. Not that they would guess that. I just happened to know, being the creature tormenting them and all.

I leapt off the cab of the truck and landed in its bed. The small truck shook under my weight, causing the couple to flinch at yet another reminder that I was very real and not likely to vanish. My nails had grown at record speed since I crossed the Veil, stretching to foreboding black claws I clicked together as I neared them. Propping

9

one stylish boot on the tailgate, I leaned in and rested my elbow on my knee.

"There was a show not long ago hosted by a man named Ambrose Graves … who has since gone toes up. In this little program, he tormented—oh, I'm sorry—*talked* to ghosts. Do you know of it?"

Steve flinched as if I'd slapped him, rapidly blinking in his attempt to make sense of any of this. "TV? You're talking about a television show?"

I hitched one brow in mild amusement. "I tried to use small words. Did they still go over your head?"

Shaking his head, Steve stammered, "N-no… I know of it. It was called Host Ghost, or something."

Casey pulled her head away from his chest, her cheeks stained with the tracks of her tears. "*Ghost Host*. It was called *Ghost Host*."

Once more I clicked my nails together. "Very good. And did the show end when Ambrose…?" Trailing off, I dragged one finger across my throat, creating the illusion of my flesh splitting open to allow black sludge to course down the front of me. The theatrics weren't mandatory, but it drove the point home that this was more than a trick of the light.

Poor Casey squealed and buried her head against Steve's chest.

"It has a new host! Some chick!" The words slipped from Steve's lips fast and furious, as if that would somehow prevent further ugliness from unfolding.

Sweet, simple boy. I had no intention of stopping until I saw this through. Blubbering wouldn't change that.

"*Name*," I demanded. "Who is she?"

Steve looked down at Casey, his eyes widening in panic at his own ineptness. "I... I don't know. I never watched that shit because I don't believe..." He trailed off, afraid to finish that sentence out of fear of insulting me.

"In ghosts?" I teased. A wave of my hand and the gore vanished as if it had never been.

Steve's chin trembled, yet he battled to stand tall.

To his great relief, Casey was bold enough to intervene once more. "Her name is Summer Raiz. She's good, very open and positive. All love ..." her voice wavered, a fresh sob shaking her shoulders, "... and light."

"Then I'm sure it will be quite the treat when you reach out to her. Tell her what happened here. Describe what you've seen. Say whatever it takes to get her and her camera crew here," I purred in a barely concealed threat.

"And if we can't? What if we can't get through to her or she won't listen?" Steve's chest puffed in what would have read as challenge were his knees not knocking together.

11

In one motion, I bounded out of the truck bed and planted myself before them. The instant the soles of my boots connected with the dirt, I allowed my earthly body to be seen. A true horror show of decay and rot in all its many facets.

Steve stifled a dry heave.

Casey fainted.

I smirked in victory. "Find a way. Make it convincing. Because, as you can see, I'm not some ghost locked to one location. I can leave here... and I will. Do as I ask, or I will find you." Leaning closer, I allowed them to see my putrefied flesh rotting away to expose my jaw bone beneath. "And I will see to it this face is the last thing you see before your eyes close each and every night."

Casey twitched from where she lay unconscious on the ground.

Steve whimpered and pissed himself.

Still, neither moved.

Dropping my voice to a whisper, I jerked my head in the direction of the truck. "Now is your chance to escape."

Gathering what remained of his wits, Steve scooped Casey up in his arms and sprinted for the truck. Without my thrall holding it, the vehicle was able to peel out without hesitation.

Reverting to my ghoulishly fabulous form, I watched them skid onto the road and blaze towards town. "Scurry off and bring back anyone who will listen. Eventually... they'll force my father to return."

Chapter Two

"She basically boot stomped me back across the Veil!" Tempest raged as she marched through the halls of Legba Manor with Sparrow following closely behind.

The Queen's Lady-in-waiting held a raven-feather skirt, patiently waiting for the Queen to pause in her rants long enough to change for her guests. "Surely, she meant no insult, Your Majesty."

Coming to an abrupt halt, Tempest spun on the pale-faced beauty. "Meant no insult? She kicked me out of her hotel! I don't care where you come from or how you were raised, slamming the door in someone's face is the universal sign for *you don't have to go home but you can't stay here.*"

Sparrow nodded in agreement while opening the skirt to allow the Queen to step into it. She shimmied it up over Tempest's black leggings and tied the corset laces between her hip bones in the back. "Feeling insulted is justified, My Queen. I simply worry there may be more details playing into this than we may be privy to."

Skirt in place, Tempest shrugged off her over-sized sweater and allowed Sparrow to dress her in a metallic silver bodice adorned with jewels. "I should have pointed out when we started this conversation that I would be speaking purely from emotion, meaning logic and common sense have no place here."

Sparrow gave a light trill of laughter. "Of course, Your Majesty. I will hate her right along with you, if that is what you need at the moment." With the Queen in her skirt and bodice, Sparrow tended to the smaller details such as fixing a necklace that dripped with rubies around Tempest's throat and straightening her crown.

"We don't hate Malaria," Tempest grumbled. "We love that bull-headed snob. That's why it's so upsetting that she took off her ring. Now, even if she comes to her senses, she can't get back. I understand her wanting to protect Carnage Crossing, but not at the expense of herself. There has to be another way to save the island besides self-sacrifice."

"I hate to rush you," Gideon, the Queen's Consort, poked his head out of the throne room, his handsome face folded in a grimace, "but you have a lengthy list of people here to see you, *mo bhanrigh*."

Tempest's shoulders sagged, her gaze drifting skyward. "Of course we do, because the entire island has gone mad. What do we have today?"

16

Gideon glanced from his beloved Queen to Sparrow and back again, as if questioning if it was a good time to unleash the current laundry list of demands.

Sparrow could only offer a shrug. "I could freeze at literally any moment. I'm not the best person to form an alliance with in these sort of matters."

"Fair enough," Gideon chuckled. Stepping closer to his love, the Consort took the Queen's hand and pressed a kiss between her knuckles. "Before I begin, let me remind you that you don't need to take all of this on at once."

"And yet I'll be expected to," Tempest sighed.

Gideon gave her hand a quick squeeze of comfort. "Enyo says people aren't eating. Haven't in days, in fact. That could be adding to the hallucinations. This claim was seconded by the staff of the Afterlife Club, stating they haven't had a customer in days. Ember has a full stock of soothing sticks; no one is purchasing them to ease their Witching Hours. Which means..."

Tempest dragged her tongue over her top teeth. "They're in so much pain, they know even soothing sticks won't help."

The corners of Gideon's lips sank into a downward C. "Speaking of pain, there is one person who requested a private audience with you."

"Is that my cue?" Doctor Despair popped out wearing a manic grin.

Tempest dropped her chin to her chest, pinching the bridge of her nose between her thumb and forefinger. "Of course, you're here. Why wouldn't you be? What can I do for you, Despair?"

The doctor shifted his weight from one foot to the other. The chaotic mess of his hair had been half-heartedly brushed back to feign some semblance of tidiness. Bless him, he was trying... kind of. "Your Majesty, I'm bombarded daily with people who are rotting and falling apart, yet they refuse to eat, drink, or tend to their well-being in any way."

"Yeah, I hear there's a lot of that going around." Tempest took his words in and chewed on the proper way to respond. "I hate myself for saying this, but right now there is no other way. Doctor Despair, I give you permission to handle their claims in the no-nonsense approach for which you're known."

Despair's spine straightened. "You don't mean..."

Tempest felt the hint of a smile tugging at the corners of her lips. "Remind them they are, in fact, past tense and then move on to the next patient."

Practically bouncing on the balls of his feet, Despair stabbed one finger in the air. "You're dead! Next! Yes, Your Majesty, I will relay this message at once."

Before the Queen could take it back, he skipped off, happy to once again be able to deliver medical advice with his own flair for not giving a damn.

"That's one appeased, an entire population to go." Tempest craned her neck to the side, taking in the throne room crowded with people buzzing in anticipation of the demands they were eager to lay at her feet.

Stepping in front of her, Gideon pulled the door shut to block out the noise. "I take it that it didn't go well with Malaria?"

Throwing her hands up, Tempest let them fall to her sides with a slap. "She basically bitch-slapped me with the Veil."

"That's a bad trip." Gideon linked his pinkie finger with that of the overwhelmed Queen. "Does that mean the Veil is shut and Malaria is on her own?"

Jaw tensed, Tempest shook her head. "I can't bring myself to close it with her out there. It goes without saying that she's a monumental pain in the ass, but... she's family. I can't leave her behind."

"I'll let your guests know you'll be in momentarily, shall I?" Sparrow bowed her head in a show of respect, then ducked behind them to disappear into the throne room.

Tempest and Gideon waited for the door to ease shut before they continued.

"You're needed here, my love." The Consort gathered his Queen in his arms, her body instinctively molding to his. "I can venture back and try to persuade her, if it suits you?"

Tempest shook her head, catching her crown as it slipped in the process. "No. It should be me. I just need to go back and try to reason with her."

Gideon curled one finger under her chin and raised Tempest's face to his. "You take everything on yourself, and don't have to. There is another option... if you're open to it."

Catching hold of Gideon's hand, Tempest begrudgingly backed up a step. "I appreciate you looking out for me, but it really is for the best. I'm not sure anyone else can get through to her. I mean, who would we send? Bones? The ghoul that perfected the art of self-sacrifice for an unnecessary cause?"

"I... was thinking more about our new arrival." Gideon offered the Queen a sheepish grin.

Tempest blinked up at him, unsure if she heard him right. "You can't be serious. He only just arrived! He's had no time to process any of this at all."

"And that's what makes him the perfect bloke for the task. He hasn't adjusted yet, which means he still has one foot planted in the land of the living... so to speak."

"We don't know the truth behind their relationship together." Tempest pressed her lips into a firm line. "All we know is that they met at some point, which may work against us. She has the people skills of a starved alligator."

"I'm well aware of that." Gideon traced Tempest's jawline with one knuckle. "But you, My Queen, need to understand that she was there at his final moment. The two may have some unfinished business that could help our cause. For the sake of Malaria... for the sake of Carnage Crossing... we have to try."

"And if he can't convince her to come home?"

Gideon kept his hand on the small of her back, offering the comfort of his embrace. "Then, we will have no choice but to seal off the Veil... and Malaria will truly be a lost soul.

Chapter Three

Lost souls don't realize they're in a prison of their own creation. So fixated are they on their unfinished business that they fail to see the world around them. Everything else fades away, trapping them with their own ugly thoughts. What's the point of these flowery sentiments? To explain just how alone I was.

More restless spirits than I could count wandered the halls of the inn, caught in an endless loop of their last tortured moments of life, all searching for a way out that didn't exist. Meaning they weren't much for small talk. I walked among them like a shadow, unseen and ineffectual.

Uncle Nathaniel's victims running from a version of him created by their own fear.

A construction worker falling from the roof while the structure was being framed.

A man at the bar of the Lost and Found getting in a brawl with another customer, only to fall and crack his skull against the marble countertop.

One I couldn't quite decipher who was simply a little boy crying in the hall, asking nonexistent people if they had seen his mommy.

Then there was the cherub-faced girl choking on candy and the sweet, simple-minded giant who was hung after the horrible accident.

Death wasn't new to me.

I lived in a town built by it.

But this was different.

This was isolation in the middle of a crowded room.

Abandonment in a place that once felt like home.

I had never experienced anything so lonely.

Since arriving, I hadn't slept for more than short bursts at a time. There was a reason for that, which went beyond the wailings of the damned. Whenever drowsiness crept in, whenever my head bobbed and my blinks grew long... *she* appeared.

The Dark Lady.

That was what I had come to call the nightmarish apparition.

Nothing could hurt me here, which was one of the benefits of being dead.

24

But that didn't mean I couldn't be terrified to the very core of my being.

That was where this mysterious entity excelled.

The first time I saw her I was looking in the mirror in the indoor pool's locker room, dragging a brush through my tangled hair. Yawning between heavy blinks, my plan after a little self-care was to find one of the many beds in the hotel to catch a few hours of sleep. Then... something flickered in the corner of my vision, drawing my eye to the reflection of the tiled room behind me. A shadow. A movement. Darkness seeped in from the furthest corners of the room, pooling and stretching into a human-like form. It disappeared and reappeared in eerie flashes. Elongated limbs. Tattered rags for clothing. Hair hanging in a stringy, matted mess. Her features were undistinguishable, her eyes nothing more than grey blurs, as if smudged by a dirty eraser.

I dropped the brush into the sink in front of me, my fingers curling around the edge of the porcelain base as if I was preparing to rip it from the wall and throw it at her. I steeled my spine... only to have my voice betray me by wavering. "Save the creepy show for the living, friend."

Her lips moved, a barely audible chant slipping out. *"There's no escape. There's no escape. There's no escape."* As she repeated the ominous sentiment, her features began to take shape. Almond-shaped brown eyes. Heart-bowed lips. Scars down one side of her face. As I watched in aghast horror, she transformed... into me. Only when the last detail was in place did she turn her head slowly to meet my wide-eyed stare. A malicious smile coiled at the corners of her lips. "It's already too late."

My gaze flicked back to my own reflection and a scream tore from my lungs. My features were indistinguishable. My eyes... grey blurs, as if smudged out by a dirty eraser.

Shoving off the sink, I sprinted for the door. My feet slapped against the Spanish tile floor as I dashed across the lobby as fast as my legs could carry me. Skidding around the front desk, I escaped into the office and slammed the door behind me. With shaking hands, I clicked the deadbolt into place. I was well aware that locked doors meant shockingly little to ghosts, but in that moment I needed to hear that *click*.

Backing away from the door, I risked a glance at the mirror Gizmo had hung beside her desk to allow her to check her appearance before stepping out amongst her guests. I was me. I was back. But I would be avoiding mirrors in this realm from that point on... just in case.

And that was only my first run-in with her. In the days that followed, I would be on the brink of sleep when I saw her skitter up the walls of my room. Or I would wake up to find her hovering, suspended, in the space above me. Time and again, she tormented me.

Bone-chilling dread scared me away from sleep. Finding musty coffee beans in the pantry, I ground them into a potent elixir that fueled my days and long nights. Exhaustion could kill the living. Thankfully, I didn't fall into that category. That being the case, I gave up sleep entirely. Instead, I was fueled by coffee and vengeance. Rest would come when I returned to Carnage Crossing.

For now, I needed to do whatever it took to draw my father there and ensure he never hurt anyone ever again. With that in mind, I sat at the bar of Lost and Found and flavored my stale black coffee with a splash of Scotch. I tuned out the screams of the dead and waited for daybreak. Kurt Crane would come. One way or another, I would see to that. Then, I would burn this place to the ground with him inside.

Justice would be done.

Souls would be freed.

And I could go home.

Only then, safely back in Carnage Crossing, would I allow myself to mourn Finnick. The sound of his laughter. The way he fiddled with his dice. The casual way he flicked his hair from his eyes. Had he never met me, he would still be alive.

I'm sorry, Finnick. I failed you. But I promise you… he will pay.

Chapter Four

Summer Raiz blew into the Crane's Roost Inn like a gentle breeze on a scorching day. Her very presence seemed to fling open the doors and cast warm beams of light into the darkest corners of the inn. Arms thrown out wide, her clothes were comprised of flowing layers of brightly colored, airy fabrics that danced around her with every movement. Her hair was a wild mass of auburn curls that haloed around her heart-shaped face. An attentive crowd followed in her footsteps, eagerly awaiting her directions. Cameramen. The costuming department. Directors. Producers. Assistants. Caterers. Boom operators. They all lingered close by, ready to attend to her every whim.

She didn't wait long to give them work to do. Planting herself in front of the empty fountain in the foyer, her cool gaze swept the room. "Put a bushel of rosemary on either side of the entrance. I don't want any negative energy to invade this space." Filling her lungs to capacity, she exhaled a sigh of appreciation. "It's simply stunning, isn't it?"

"Yes, ma'am," one of her many yes-men uttered with manufactured sincerity. "Where shall we set up the cameras and sound equipment?"

Raising one hand beside her head, Summer wagged a finger in the air. "No equipment of any sort. Not yet. Tonight, we let the spirits know we're not a threat by presenting them with a generous offering." Dropping her hands in front of her, she counted off her list on her fingers. "I need chalices of wine placed in the four corners of this room. Next to them, put offerings of fresh produce and an exquisite collection of cheeses. We want the spirits here to know we mean them no harm, and will do *nothing* without their approval."

Hidden in the shadows of the steepled atrium above them, I watched from my seat on the ledge of one of the stained-glass windows. Were any of them to look up, they wouldn't catch a glimpse of me until I deemed it so.

And it wasn't time.

Not yet.

Instead, I kept still and watched them prepare their pointless offerings.

Leave it to the living to think the dead could be swayed with food and wine.

Although... as I watched a full-bodied Merlot being poured into a golden chalice, I had to admit my mouth suddenly went dry. Not that I planned to partake. I needed my wits about me. If my efforts were too subtle, I risked them being ignored. Yet if I went too grand, they could run screaming from this place and never return. I only had one chance to get this right.

Once everything inside was aligned to meet Summer's exact specifications, her team busied themselves unloading the trucks. Entire yurts were assembled in minutes. Bohemian style rugs were rolled out to add a homey air. Vintage-style furnishings were carefully arranged. In a few short hours, they created an inviting little mobile community I fully intended to terrorize. Eventually.

But time was the one thing I had in spades, and I was fully prepared to wait for the perfect moment to strike. For the time being, I would let them settle in and get comfortable. Allow them to be lulled into a false sense of security. Then, I'd creep in and present them with the kind of paranormal evidence that simply couldn't be ignored. Once they saw something real, something truly remarkable, they would need to contact the property owner to get permission to air any footage they filmed. Which, of course, was none other than dear ole Dad. If all went well, he would be forced to travel here in just a few days' time—thanks to the increasingly volatile events I would see to it would be happening—to face all the sins of his past that he'd left roosting here at the inn.

Making the decision to wait until after dark to make my first contact, I melded into the wall behind me. Through my will alone, I transported my essence to the largest suite in the resort. It was affectionately named the Love Nest by my great grandmother, and it had the best view of all the rooms. One rounded out wall allowed for windows on three sides that looked out at the dense woods surrounding the inn. There was a time when every tree was trimmed to perfection, the lawn painstakingly mowed. Now bare branches clawed towards the heavens. Thorny vines and foliage braided together across the ground, acting as a natural barrier to warn away the living. Heavy clouds hung overhead, casting a gray hue to the otherwise sepia pallet.

The entire landscape made me ache for the exquisite green and purple swirling skyline of Carnage Crossing, where the streets were filled with residents buzzing about in regal styles of my own design.

But, if I was being truthful with myself, what I missed most... was *him*.

Finnick.

I thought his name and my mind manifested him.

Gentle fingers traced down my arms, his warm breath teasing over the curve of my neck.

"You had to know I would never go far," he murmured against my ear.

Closing my eyes, I leaned into him and welcomed the feel of his strong arms enveloping me. "I don't like it here without you."

Nuzzling closer, he pressed a kiss into my hair. "I know. But you have work to do. Don't worry, I'll be with you all the while."

Turning to face him, I stared deep into his mahogany gaze, trying my best to focus only on what was right in front of me. "What if drawing my father in takes too long and I'm stuck here? What then?"

Finnick brushed the tip of my nose with his. "Then, we will wander these halls hand-in-hand until the building crumbles around us and turns to dust."

"Tell me this isn't all a mistake. That it hasn't been for nothing." Feeling the sting of inky black tears welling behind my eyes, I rose on my tiptoes to treat myself to the sweet taste of his lips.

He wiped my tears away with the pads of his thumbs. "None of this has been for nothing. It brought us together."

Together.

Together...

But we weren't.

Not anymore.

And that was enough to shatter the illusion.

I couldn't taste his lips.

Couldn't feel his touch.

Couldn't smell the lemongrass body wash he took from the hotel room we shared, that he went on to use... until the day he died.

Stumbling back a step, I watched as my illusion self-corrected to the horrifying truth.

In a blink, his eyes morphed to a lifeless gray. All color drained from his complexion. Icicles crystalized in his hair. His lips were kissed with a deep blue shade, brought on by the freezer in which his body had been unceremoniously dropped.

As the whole horrid scene came rushing back, a noose of anguish and guilt tightened around my throat.

Finnick's head tilted, his haunting gaze wide and unblinking. "You led me right to him," he rasped, judgment dripping from each word. "I never should have been there, but you marched me right into that maniac's office. I had a life in New York, a quaint little family business and a mother who loved me. We never got to say goodbye... *because of you.*"

I glanced down at his hand still on my arm, watching in horror as rot set in. His fingers locked in a rigid claw. Skin cracked, crumbling away to reveal bone beneath.

Squeezing my eyes shut, I shook my head. "It's not real. None of this is real."

"No, it's not," he whispered against my cheek, his hot breath tainted by the stench of death. "And it never will be again, because you failed, Malaria. That's what you do. The family you tried to help, how did that go? Ole Timmy boy ended up with a bullet between his eyes, while mommy and daughter were entombed in cement... because of you. Your ex-boyfriend, Dexter? He chose death over a simple conversation with you. And me? I cared for you. May even have grown to love you. But you let me die... just... like... this." His shoulders shook with hacking coughs, spittle foaming at his lips as he replayed the moment he was poisoned for his horrified audience of one.

I knew it wasn't real. I was torturing myself, nothing more. Still, I dove to catch his head as he slumped to the floor. Cradling his upper body in my lap, I stroked his hair until the image of him faded away... having never truly been there at all.

That was when I saw her peering back at me from the vanity mirror. Lurking. Waiting. Tempting me to let my guard down long enough for her to slink back in. That faceless being of darkness and despair, flickering in and out of focus.

Pushing off the floor, I rose to my feet on legs that threatened to buckle beneath me. *"I'm not going to cower from you!"* I screamed my throat raw. *"My days of living in fear died when I did. In case you didn't notice, I have nothing left to lose!"*

"Room thirteen." She croaked those two words in a demonic whisper... then vanished from sight.

Throwing my arms out wide, I let them fall to my sides in a slap. *"What does that mean? Go to room thirteen? Stay away from it? Even a thumbs up or down would have been helpful!"*

My shouts made it as far as the walls, reminding me I was all alone.

In that instant, the words echoed through my mind of the conversation I had staged with Finnick that seemed like a warning from my own subconscious.

"What if drawing my father in takes too long and I'm stuck here? What then?"

"Then we will wander these halls until the building crumbles around us and turns to dust."

But the only *we* in this scenario were the other trapped spirits.

Still, I couldn't let up. It was a risk I had to take… to finally bring Kurt Crane down.

Chapter Five

Some hauntings are just more fun than others. That thing with the frisky couple? That was simply a good time. In Steven's case, a pants-wetting good time. I never had any intention of hurting them, but had carte blanche to scare the hell out of them. I don't care who you are, that's fun.

But this? This was different. I didn't want Summer to run. Terrified to her core wasn't an option. I wanted her to have the kind of ethereal experience she would want to share with others... mainly her hordes of *Ghost Host* viewers. For that to happen, I had to play nice.

I don't know if you've picked this up about me, but in normal situations... I don't do nice. Resting bitch face was my default setting. Even so, I was goal-oriented enough to try my best not to take things too far and traumatize anyone.

From the atrium I watched and waited for nightfall, allowing darkness to steal over their camp. One by one the crew settled in for the night and clicked off their lanterns. A peaceful hush fell, signaling the time had come. I moved through the camp as little more than a chilling breeze. Passing through the canvas flap of Summer's makeshift door, the fabric gave barely a flutter.

I won't lie, I pulled up short at the spectacle I found inside. This was no mere pop-up tent. Oh, no. Girlfriend proved she was the star here with the accommodations she required. A walnut four-poster bed had been trucked in just for her. The cloud of pillows and blankets nestled on it were all white satin and faux fur. Truth be told, I respected her sense of extravagance. What was the point of existing, if not to revel in moments of ultimate comfort? While the others had generators and battery-operated lanterns, Summer had pillar candles in ornate, brass candelabras positioned around the quaint space. Thankfully all had been extinguished for the night, allowing me the perfect opportunity.

Hidden from sight to the living, I inched closer to the side of her bed. Crouching beside the sleeping host, my will allowed my left hand to become corporeal. Slowly, I dragged the knuckle of my index finger across her cheek, down her neck, and over her clavicle. I stopped before crossing the line of venturing anywhere near her cleavage... I didn't want her to think this was *that* kind of haunting.

40

As Summer stirred, I made my hand vanish once more and allowed myself to meld with the shadows. A roll of my fingers allowed three candles by her bed to flicker to life, their glow causing light to dance up the walls of the yurt.

Summer sat up with a yawn and stretched her arms out wide. In between heavy blinks, she noticed the glowing candles. Her head tilted with mild interest. Throwing back her covers, she swung her feet over the side of her mattress and let her toes sink into the thick nap of the sunshine yellow rug. Without hesitation, she padded over to blow them out.

I lifted my hand, meaning to levitate a candle before her eyes. Before I could, she gave another yawn, scratched her boob inside her over-sized t-shirt, and flopped back down on the bed. Grumbling my annoyance, I snapped my fingers to reignite the wicks. Summer rolled to her side, her face a question mark. Grabbing the mason jar full of water from her wicker bedside table, she used the water to extinguish what she believed to be a stubborn flame and returned to bed.

Shoulders sagging, I rolled my eyes. "This would be so much easier if I could go ahead and traumatize you. Keep it up and I'm going to give into temptation, rip my face off, and let you watch me pop my eyeballs out of their sockets."

Oblivious to my warning, Summer eased back down onto her feather-topped mattress and snuggled under her blankets. A glance around the space and I readjusted my plan. Rolling both wrists, I lit every candle in her yurt, brightening the space to a midday glow.

Summer sat up with a start, clutching her comforter tightly to her chest. "Hello? Who's there?"

I raised my hands and the flames licked higher, clawing towards the ceiling.

"We mean you no harm," Summer tried again, her spine straightening with purpose. "We just want to make contact, and—if you'll allow us—learn your story. Would you gift us that honor?"

Dropping my hands, I allowed the candles to flicker out.

Scrambling out of her bed, Summer grabbed a sapphire kimono from a clothing rack beside her bed and flung it around her shoulders. "Wait! Don't go! Just give me a sign of what I can do to earn your trust and put you at ease."

Form still not visible to her eye, I pulled back the canvas door far enough to give her a clear view of the front of the Inn. Glowing pillar candles now lit the way to the once grand entrance because I willed it so. Every long-dimmed light in the hotel now burned bright as chords of old-timey jazz music beckoned her inside...

Chapter Six

As hauntings went, I kept this one incredibly tame. With all the spirits trapped within the hotel, I had a full cast of characters at my disposal and used every last one. More accurately, an illusion of them, as the real thing was torturing their own psyche elsewhere. The end result was a spectral glimpse of what the once fabulous resort had looked like in its heyday. Old school glitz and glamour... brought to Summer from the Great Beyond.

Upbeat jazz music wafted out of a nonexistent record player in the Lost and Found Lounge. The eerie blue silhouette of a young couple danced along doing the Lindy Hop. Heads thrown back in laughter, the vaporous forms of the producer and his starlet strolled through the lobby arm-in-arm. A giant man with the mind of a child played hide and seek with a little girl with a lollipop in her mouth. Summer's eyes widened to goose eggs as a bellhop wheeling a cart full of luggage paused to tip his hat in her direction. From the indoor pool on one side to the lounge on the other, the entire vast space had come alive with the vivacious dead.

Jaw hanging slack, Summer turned in a slow circle and took it all in. Her eyes, wide and unblinking, reflected the glow of each apparition sauntering past her. Just as I hoped, she didn't seem fearful, but awestruck at the scene before her.

Noticing that the starlet who checked her lipstick in a cracked mirror in the lobby cast no reflection, Summer waved her hand in front of the preening spirit's face.

"Hi ya, doll." The starlet tossed Summer a wink before sashaying back to her boyfriend's side.

An involuntary giggle bubbled from Summer's throat. "This is incredible. I've seen shimmers that I convinced myself were spirits, but *never* anything like this. *This* is concrete proof! *This*... changes everything!"

My shoulders sagged with relief. No way would she walk away from this. She wanted to show the world, and that meant reaching out to the last remaining member of my family, Daddy Dearest. Riding the wave of my victory, I rubbed the heels of my hands into my eyes to grind away that ever present exhaustion. That subtle moment where my attention wasn't one-hundred percent focused was all it took. To my absolute horror, I felt my control... slip.

Darkness tinged the corners of my vision, my blinks growing long and heavy. The world around me blurred, white-hot pain stabbing into my temples. I needed to get Summer out of the inn, but I couldn't see her through the shadows roiling and churning before my eyes.

"No, not now." Jaw locked tight, my hands curled into fists at my sides.

The Dark Lady was coming, and I couldn't protect Summer.

Hell, I couldn't protect myself.

My own illusions betrayed me, cracking at the corners.

A crimson gash split the producer's neck.

Blood dripped from the brow of the starlet from the knife embedded in her skull.

The bellhop spewed gore from his lips, caused by the pair of scissors stabbed into his throat.

A scream ripped from Summer's lungs as one after another, the ghostly spirits gave her a grisly glimpse of their final moments. My hand shot out, hoping to seize hold of her wrist and drag her out of the hellish nightmare I'd forced upon her.

Before I could grab hold, the hotel swallowed me whole. I tumbled through the floorboards, sinking to the dark, dank boiler room below. Pipes rattled as if in warning. Steam hissed from the water heater. The boiler clanged, fingers of flames darting from its grates as if beckoning me. The hotel hadn't been operational in decades. None of this could be real. But that was an argument I could convince myself of later as the temperature of the space around me rose to a stifling degree. My head swam with a disconnected feeling I couldn't shake or escape.

From the ripples of heat wafting off the boiler... *she* emerged. That dark entity with smudged out eyes and a wicked grin. She tapped her talon-like nails together at her sides as she floated towards me.

"So much fight left in you. You even dragged one of the living here for the inn to feast upon."

Paralyzed by fear, I couldn't move. Couldn't blink. The most I could muster was letting my gaze twitch in her direction as she stalked a predatory circle around me.

"Why would you sacrifice another? Isn't there enough blood on your hands already?" The Dark Lady asked with a mocking chuckle. "Gizmo. Finnick. Timothy. Sweet little Clara. And don't forget her poor mother." She clucked her long black tongue against the roof of her mouth. "You don't even remember her name, do you? You were the reason her life was snuffed out, and all she is to you is Clara's mother. How pathetically tragic."

I jerked my head in an emphatic shake. "No... please, stop."

Raising her hand beside my head, she clicked her talons together hard and fast, the sound resonating through me like nails being hammered into a coffin. "Stop what? Speaking the truth? Face it, Malaria. Just like those lost souls wandering the halls upstairs, you're never leaving this place. You think you're so different because your soul once found peace? You gave that up when you came back here. Did you think you could escape this unscathed? No one does. That's the thing about the land of the living; the cost of time here is always death. And now, you've got nothing to barter with. Perhaps you'd like to see what *your* eternity will look like, because it's coming for you with a ravenous hunger."

The room shifted around me and I found myself in the belly of the boiler. Instead of cast iron grates, its door morphed into clouded glass... just like that of the steam room I died in. Panic tightening my throat, I beat my fists against the glass. *"Don't do this! Let me out!"* The black tinged tears sliding down my cheeks instantly evaporated in the heat.

The Dark Lady tapped her nails against the other side of the door. "There's no way out. It's already too late. Whether you get your revenge or not makes no difference. From this point on, you're going to burn, Malaria. For the rest of eternity, you... will... burn."

I raised my hands in front of me and screamed as I experienced the most torturous pain of my existence for the second time. My flesh boiled and blistered, melting to the bone. The heat stole into my lungs, scorching me from the inside out. Trapped in my own eternal nightmare, I crumbled to the floor and prayed to Legba to make it end.

That was when I felt a gloriously cold chill on the back of my neck. "Malaria," a familiar voice pressed. "I need you to get up. Do you hear me?"

I fought to open my eyes, only to find my blurred vision unable to focus. "Finnick?"

"I need you to stay with me. We're going to get you out of here." He wrapped my arm around his neck and supported my weight as I fumbled to get my feet under me.

I knew he wasn't there. He couldn't be. Still, I appreciated the extra effort my subconscious was putting into this tactical means of motivation. "I'm sorry you died. I couldn't save you. Can't save anyone." The words slurred from my lips, my tongue feeling thick and swollen.

"We can talk about that, and this new defeatist attitude of yours, once we get out of here. For now, we need to move." His arm gripped tightly around my waist, pinching my skin between his fingers.

"This seems so real... so convincing." I brought my free hand up and slapped it against his cheek with more force than necessary. Subtlety and grace weren't achievable traits in my foggy-brained state. He was cold. Freezing, in fact. "Cold because he's not really here," I mumbled to myself as he hurried me up the stairs.

"I don't know why you came back here." Finnick flung open the door at the top of the stairs, which creaked on its hinges in protest. "But you need to leave now while there's still time."

Chaos had exploded in the foyer. Every spirit stuck in the hotel was simultaneously experiencing their witching hour. Trapped in the middle of this gruesome pandemonium, Summer was jostled from one grisly scene to the next, screaming all the while.

"No!" Pushing away from Finnick, I planted one foot firmly on my own. Then, the other. "This isn't right. It's not part of the plan."

I felt Finnick's hand slipping away from the small of my back. "Malaria, please! *Promise me*! You have to leave the inn!"

Brushing off his pleas, I glanced back in time to see him vanish from sight. Just as I thought he would, because he'd never truly been there at all. Shaking off a crushing wave of melancholy, I cast out my intentions and took a corporeal form as I rushed to Summer's aid.

"Take my hand!" I stretched my hand towards hers, shouting to be heard over her ear-piercing shrieks. "I'll get you out of here."

"You're real!" She caught my hand and squeezed it in a white-knuckled grip. "Help me, *please!*"

Mirroring the pose my illusion of Finnick ushered me along in, I wrapped Summer's arm around my neck and darted for the door. "I've got you. It's going to be okay."

She buried her face against my shoulder, muttering sentiments of gratitude. "Thank you. Thank you so much. I froze up. I couldn't move."

The instant we burst out into the night, Summer's crew caught sight of their flustered boss and rushed over to help.

"Summer!"

"What happened?"

"Are you okay?"

"When did you go in there? And why alone?"

"I wasn't alone," Summer managed a wavering stance all on her own and turned to face me. "*She* was there, and she helped me."

But I was already gone, my presence once more cloaked from the living.

Summer's brows knitted together tightly, her mouth opening and shutting in confusion. "There was a dark-haired woman who found me and helped me out…"

While the crew exchanged nervous glances, an olive-skinned beauty with a smattering of freckles on the apples of her cheeks weaved her way through the crowd to catch hold of Summer's hand. "That's it," she stated, trying to drag the show host in the direction of their line of cars. "We're leaving. You heard what those teenagers said. The spirits here are restless and malicious. Now you're being led around by some mysterious ghost chick? Nope. Let the others pack up, or just leave everything behind. Either way, we need to take this as a sign and *go*."

Summer planted her feet firm and yanked her arm away. "You can't be serious! How many episodes have we filmed where we made a big deal out of the tiniest noise or shimmer, all the while feeling like hacks? *Real* proof of the paranormal is in that hotel." She jabbed her upturned palm in the direction of the inn. "This is it! This is what we've been waiting for! If we can get even a fraction of what I saw tonight on camera, we can step out of Ambrose's shadow and make a name for ourselves doing the kind of show we want. The kind of show where we help restless spirits like those in there find peace. This is it, Sami. This is our chance!"

Freckle-faced Sami puffed her cheeks and expelled an exasperated breath through pursed lips. "The first sign of trouble, and we're out of here. Do you hear me?"

Summer grabbed the girl's upper arms and planted a kiss on her cheek. "Yes! Thank you! But there won't be any more trouble. The spirits want us here. They know we can help. That's why one of them came to my rescue. And I won't let them down. Find the owner of the hotel. Put me in touch with them. We need permission to roll cameras. What happens here will change everything, and we can't afford to make any mistakes."

Chest puffed with renewed purpose, I turned back to the hotel. There, in the second story window, I saw Finnick's silhouette staring down at me. He wasn't anything more than the haunted longing of my heart. But tonight... he was all I had.

Chapter Seven

I was lost.

In time.

In this place.

How long it had been, I couldn't say.

My coherency came in flashes.

The time between them nothing but blackness.

I remembered walking back into Crane's Roost, looking for something...

What that was, I couldn't recall.

Since then, I had been swallowed by darkness that spat me out at its leisure.

Was I haunting the hotel, or was the hotel haunting me?

"You have to get out of here, Malaria. Leave Crane's Roost. I'm begging you."

The voice, which seemed to come from everywhere and nowhere all at once, sounded concerned. Terrified.

My own subconscious warning me? Perhaps.

I'd get out soon. The end was in sight. For now, I needed to focus... just a little bit longer.

A scream snapped me back to the here and now. Twilight had fallen, marking the passing of a new day. How many of them I missed, I couldn't say. Cameramen and crew members filled the lobby, yet their equipment had been all but forgotten. They stood frozen and transfixed. Eyes white and unblinking. Arms limp at their sides. Each unseeing gaze was locked on the center of the room where Summer huddled in fear as the Dark Lady moved towards her in an eerily fluid gait.

"Please, I'm begging you! I only wanted to help!" Tears streaked down Summer's face, her entire body trembling from the force of her sobs. *"Somebody help me, please!"*

The Dark Lady tilted her head, feigning interest. Raising one blackened hand, she clicked her talon-like nails across the marble front desk as she sauntered past it. "There's no escape. It's already too late."

No. I couldn't let this play out. If Summer was hurt—or worse—before she reached out to my father, all I had done would be for nothing. For reasons I couldn't understand, my legs felt like leaden weights. It took every ounce of strength I had to force them forward. I battled for every step, knowing if the only help I could offer was positioning myself between Summer and the ghoul, that was what I had to do.

Summer's screams reached a fevered pitch. The tendons of her neck bulged from the strain, her muscles locked rigid with fear. The tip of the Dark Lady's nail brushed a strand of the show host's hair, twirling it around the end of her extended digit.

"Leave her alone!" Even as I growled the words, I knew I was too late.

I'd never make it to her in time, not when my own body seemed to be working against me.

"I will!" Summer blubbered, shrinking further away. "I'll leave and never step foot in here again. You have my word. Just please, *please*, let me go!"

Odd that she thinks I'm talking to her when such a ghastly threat is…

My thought trailed off, my attention torn away by the dusty Victorian mirror hanging just outside the Lost and Found Lounge.

No.

That's not right.

It can't be.

I glanced down at my hand to see one silky strand of Summer's hair twirled around the tip of my finger. Shaking it off, I stumbled back. Black hands. Talon nails. It couldn't be! Yet, there was no denying this chilling truth.

I wasn't watching the Dark Lady stalk the terrified host.

I snapped back to consciousness to catch sight of my own reflection as *I* terrorized her.

All this time, I hadn't been running from the Dark Lady.

I am her.

She was the side of my mind losing control... spiraling me into madness.

That should've been all the proof I needed to run from the Crane's Roost Inn and never look back. But I'd come too far. And now, the only thing I had to fear... was myself.

Allowing my features to release the dreadful Dark Lady façade, I turned my attention back to Summer.

"I—I remember you," she sniveled, wiping her nose on the back of her arm. "You... helped me."

"And now, you're going to help me." The gravelly rasp that seeped from my lips was foreign to my ears, just one more part of me I no longer recognized.

I offered her a hand up. When she hesitated, I rolled my fingers and Summer was lifted from the ground. With her feet dangling above the marble floor, I floated her to me. She tried to wriggle free, to throw her body weight away from me. My influence quieted her. Reaching out, I placed my hand over her heart and placed her under my thrall.

Acting of my will, she reached into the pocket of her cotton overalls and pulled out her phone. Summer clicked one button, then put the phone to her ear.

I could hear through her.

Speak through her.

Use her as my receptacle in this as my means to an end.

My father picked up on the second ring, his voice gruff with annoyance. "Damn it, I told you to do whatever you want at that hotel. Just leave me out of it! That place is a curse I'd happily be rid of!"

"Mr. Crane," I spoke through Summer. "The situation here is far more dire than we could have imagined. We need you here at once."

Kurt scoffed. "I'm a busy man, and I can assure you that will *not* be happening. You want to film your little show? Go for it. But I won't step foot in that place ever again."

"Yes you will," I dropped my voice to a menacing hiss. "Because I know the truth. Where *all* the bodies are buried, Kurt. Even the ones down there in Florida. *Everything* is going to come to light unless you come here and help me bury it… once and for all."

My father gave a humorless chuckle. "Are you threatening me, young lady? Because I promise you, you have no idea what I'm capable of."

"Oh, yes. I absolutely do, and that's how I know you're going to hop the first flight here. Because that's what you do. You make problems disappear, and I intend to lay them all out for the world to see." With that, I allowed Summer to end the call and retracted my influence.

Releasing the hold over the room I'd unknowingly seized, I sank back into the darkness. This time, willfully allowing it to consume me.

Chapter Eight

I watched Summer's crew pack up and leave with detached interest. I'm sure in some dark recess of my mind I knew I should feel somewhat guilty. Whether it was intentional or not, I was the reason they were running from the hotel with their tails tucked. Even so, I couldn't bring myself to feel bad. Truth be told, I couldn't seem to feel... anything anymore.

Since making the decision to stay in Crane's Roost, my emotions had been in a constant state of turmoil. Fear. Rage. Guilt. Sorrow. Regret. Wrath. At any given moment I was being attacked by one of them or the next. Discovering I was the Dark Lady somehow muted all that. The realization seeped into my veins, freezing out anything that dared to distract me and replaced it with icy determination. Nothing in the mortal coil could sway me now. I was beyond their trappings... and I had the inn, with all its ghoulish delights, to thank for that.

"Malaria?"

The corners of my mouth curled up at the sound of Finn's voice. Why not treat myself to a tryst with the illusion of him? No longer did I need to concern myself with a darkness that may creep in if I let my guard down. I *was* that roiling blackness.

Dropping my voice to a husky whisper, I wet my lips and glanced his way. "Of all the hauntings here, you are by far my favorite. But I must say, you're wearing far too much clothing. We should really do something about that."

To my surprise, when I reached for the buttons of his shirt, he batted my hands away. "Malaria, I need you to hear me. *Truly* hear me."

Stifling an eyeroll, I played along to whatever game my subconscious was playing. "Didn't peg you as the type to play hard to get."

Catching hold of my hand, he gave it a tight squeeze. "I need you to *see me*. Can you do that?"

I scoffed at the lunacy of such a question. "Of course I can. Wait, is this you fishing for a compliment? Okay, your hair seems less of a chaotic mess today. How's that?"

Finnick winced, then physically shook off the insult. "Passive aggressively rude, yet not at all out of character. Still, not what I'm talking about. I'm *here*, Malaria. Actually here, standing in front of you right now. I've been here for a while, but every time I've tried to get through to you, you get lost deeper in your own mind. I was the one who dragged you from the basement. And now I'm here, holding your hand and begging you to *see me*."

I tried to pull away, only for Finnick to tighten his grip. "No, that's not possible. I watched you die in my father's office. There's no way your spirit could have found its way here."

One corner of his mouth tugged back in a half-grin. "Is that a fact? Well, to play devil's advocate, you didn't die here, either. Yet, here you are."

I shook my head, trying to deny the truth staring back at me. "I was in Carnage Crossing, and had a ring that allowed me to—"

Before I could utter another word, Finnick raised his hand beside his face and tapped the green aventurine ring on his pinkie with his index finger. "Lovely little town, Carnage Crossing. Though I could do without the Screaming Well. The random shrieks will take some getting used to. I've been told there's more of them as of late, with the island in a complete state of upheaval and all. But we hope to put a stop to all that once *you* are home and we can finally close the Veil."

My brows knitted together, thoughts of home threatening to thaw a bit of my iced-over heart. "Tempest… said she was going to close it. I gave her the ring and told her to leave me behind."

Finnick's head tilted, his eyes crinkling in the corners. "And you thought she would so easily? The Queen wanted to march back here and drag you home herself, but she thought I might be a bit more convincing."

He finally dropped my hand, which granted me the freedom to take a step back... then another. Easing back influence I hadn't known I cast out, I allowed myself to see him as he was. His once peaches and cream skin was stark white and frozen. His hair was frozen in icicles that jutted off his head in every direction. Even the white suit he wore perfectly matched the icy style of his death. Pale. Frozen. Fitting, considering he died in a walk-in freezer.

"When you touched the back of my neck..." Eyes narrowing, I tried to piece together what he was saying.

He inspected his frigid hand as if seeing it for the first time. "You were burning. Locked in a self-inflicted Witching Hour—which I've learned all about since I keeled over. That's a nightmarish hell to suffer nightly."

I couldn't begin to wrap my mind around what this meant... or what I wanted it to mean. Instead, I turned the question on him. "Why did you come here? To convince me to return for the good of Carnage Crossing?"

Looping his thumbs in the pockets of his suit jacket, Finnick gave a boyish shrug. "I wanted you to know the truth, so whatever decision you make is based on all the facts."

Chewing on the inside of my cheek, I fought to keep my expression neutral. "The truth? The truth is that we shared a couple of kisses in the middle of some traumatizing shit. And now I'm supposed to do *what* with that information? Give up my dream of seeing karma give my father the bitch-slap he so richly deserves in the name of something between us that barely evolved past a crush?"

Pain flashed in Finnick's eyes, his jaw tensing with whatever sentiment he battled to hold back. "There's no reason to purposely be cruel. It was more than that, and you know it."

Dragging my tongue over my lower lip, I chuckled. "When the Queen sent you here, did she tell you how I booted her back beyond the Veil? It took shockingly little effort on my part, thanks to the Algea. Now..." I brushed a bit of lint from his shoulder and straightened his necktie, "I *am* the darkness that infects this hotel. Everything within these walls obeys my every whim." As I uttered the words, the candles left on the vanity table of the suite by Summer's crew sparked to light. "The whispers in the halls speak my every thought."

Finnick's head snapped towards the door as an eerie chant echoed down the hall.

"There's no escape. It's already too late."

The doorknobs of every room shook and rattled as if someone—or some*thing*—was trying to break through. Disembodied hands stretched from the plaster walls in search of escape.

"Every shadow that moves at the corner of your vision does so at *my* command." I moved around him in a slow circle, whispering the words against his ear. "There may be other spirits trapped on these grounds, but *I* am the being who truly haunts these halls. And I have no intention of stopping until the job I came to do is done."

If any of this unnerved him in any way, Finnick refused to let it show. "Then what?"

My mouth fell open. To my great regret, no snappy comeback tumbled out. Mainly, because I had been so laser focused on my father I hadn't allowed myself to think beyond his betrayal. In place of an answer, I turned the question on him. "What do you mean, then what? Then, he rots in hell like the demon he is."

Finnick closed the distance between us, moving in body-skimming close. "I meant what happens to you? Do you think whatever nastiness has rooted itself in your veins is just going to let you go? Take a look at yourself, Malaria." He jabbed his up-turned palm at the vanity mirror. "Do you look like you're in control? Is this something you think you can just walk off?"

I followed his gaze to the mirror. My eyes narrowed and head tilted in fascination at the dark entity staring back at me. The inky blackness that tipped my fingers stretched up my arms in forking veins. Lack of sleep and nourishment had sunk my features. My hair hung in filthy strands that clung to my cheeks. The light behind my eyes was dim and lifeless. And, in the worst insult of all, my once stylish ensemble was now grimy and tattered. The Dark Lady appearance wasn't a façade I was shrugging on and off as I thought. It had taken me over, melding into a macabre mask that made it impossible to tell where the Algea ended and I began.

My black-tipped fingers lifted, brushing over the curve of my sunken cheeks. "All this is necessary to bring my father down. Then, I can cast out the sorrow-sucker and return home to Carnage Crossing."

Stepping closer, Finnick placed his hand on my shoulder. "Do you have any idea at all how to do that? You're losing yourself, Malaria, to whatever this thing is. When the day comes that you're done with *it*, there's no guarantee it will be done with *you*."

Turning his way on the ball of my foot, I placed a gentle hand to his frozen cheek. "I appreciate you coming here, and I wish things were different. But I can't stop now. I can't allow Kurt Crane to hurt anyone else."

Finnick's lips parted with a pop. "About that – there's one more vital piece of information you need to know."

Features folding into a frown, I shook my head. "No, there isn't. Nothing you can say will change my mind. Go back to Carnage Crossing, Finnick. Tell the Queen you did your best. Encourage her to close the Veil, secure in the knowledge that nothing any of you could've done would have swayed me."

"Please, just listen, if not for yourself than for—"

I cut him off with a finger to his lips.

"I'm happy you get to have an afterlife in Carnage Crossing, Finnick, and I sincerely hope I see you again." With that, I reached down and gave the stone on his finger a quarter turn. He vanished in a blink, back beyond the Veil.

As he faded into nothingness, I uttered a final goodbye to him… and all that I would miss on the other side.

Chapter Nine

Finnick pinwheeled back across the Veil before landing in a heap on the cobblestone street of Croaking Lane. Quickly rolling out of the way from fear of being run over by a peddle car, he dragged himself to his feet in front of Malaria's shop, Death Shroud Clothing & More. But there were no cars or people in sight. Unease prickled down his spine. The island was quiet as a tomb. All the windows were shuttered. The lamps in every home and business dimmed. Petrified something horrible had happened in his absence, Finnick sprinted around the corner to Nightshade Alley and followed it to Legba Manor.

Reaching the Queen's estate, he frantically rapped on the door.

After a wait that stretched on long enough for Finnick to fear no one would answer, Bones eased open the door. Despite being comprised of nothing but bone, somehow the seven foot tall skeleton managed to look exhausted. "Apologies, my boy. I was tending to the medical needs of the Queen and her Consort. Having long since decayed during my self-banishment, I'm the only one not suffering the pangs of life tormenting the others. I'm trying to help as many people as I can, but it feels all my efforts are for naught. Please, tell me you've returned with good news."

Finnick stalled for time by answering his question with a question. "I take it things have gotten worse?"

Dropping his chin to his chest plate, Bones gave a melancholy nod. "The Queen has taken to her bed. The wound made in her neck by the planchette has begun bleeding nonstop. Gideon can't offer her aid because he's constantly choking on gushes of water bubbling up from his gullet. The Veil must be closed. We can't wait any longer. What happened with Malaria? Did you convince her to return?"

Finnick shook his head. He could already feel the effects of life that tainted the town seeping into him. A frosty chill settled into his marrow, causing his body to convulse in shivers and his teeth to chatter. "I finally managed to break through and make contact, but it wasn't enough. She can't see past her rage at her father."

Crossing one spindly arm across his middle, Bones propped his chin on the back of his opposite hand. "I can't say I blame her. Learning your own father ordered your death must be the kind of betrayal from which a heart never recovers. That said, we can't give up. I understand the Queen doesn't want to close the Veil and leave Malaria behind, but—"

"The Queen is correct in that." Finnick's chest puffed in protective bravado. "Malaria is struggling right now, but if we just give her a little more time…"

"Her struggles do not outweigh those of the people of Carnage Crossing!" the towering skeleton boomed, pulling himself up to his full, impressive height.

Finnick raised both hands, palms out, trying to deescalate the tense situation in between the frosty tremors quaking through him. "You're right. The will of one can't outweigh the needs of many. Even so, don't you think now, more than ever, we need to show everyone on this island that we won't give up on them, no matter what? That every afterlife here is worth fighting for? I haven't been here long, but I know community is what makes Carnage Crossing truly special. If we shatter that delicate thread of civility, all that has been built here will crumble."

Bones folded his arms over his rib cage and fixed his eerie red stare on the island's newest resident. "It sounds to me like you're willing to say whatever it takes to buy yourself more time to save the girl you've grown fond of."

Eyes narrowing, Finnick tried to offer a half-grin. Unfortunately, his chattering teeth made it look more like a grimace. "Is it working?"

Bones took a threatening step closer and stabbed one digit in the newcomer's direction. "You have *one* more chance. Then, I will prop the Queen up myself and see to it that she clamps the Veil shut for all eternity... no matter what side of it you and Malaria happen to be on. Do whatever it takes to get her back here or run the risk of becoming a lost soul alongside her. Success or failure will decide your fate."

"But no pressure, right?" Hand violently shaking, Finnick caught hold of the ring on his pinkie and gave it a half-turn. A blink later, the former shop-keep vanished in an iridescent swirl of purple and green.

Only then did the door to the Queen's quarters open. Tempest appeared at the top of the stairs holding a blood soaked handkerchief to her neck. "Are you sure that was the right thing to do?"

Shaking out a fresh towel from the folded stack he'd retrieved from the Dead End Resort, Bones jogged up the stairs to change out her bandage with a fresh one. "If our goal is still to get Miss Cain home before closing the Veil, I believe the boy is our only hope. And now, we have armed him with fresh motivation. All we can do now is pray to Legba that he can find a way to convince her."

Chapter Ten

Kurt didn't come alone. Not that I thought he would. When the silver Cadillac eased to a stop in front of the hotel, my father waited patiently in the back seat for his driver/bodyguard to come around and open the door for him. Truth be told, I'd expected his lackey from the medically induced prison he called a *senior center* to accompany him. I was hoping for it, in fact. I hadn't gotten over the scarring image of watching that needle full of poison being plunged into Finnick's neck. It would have brought me great joy to watch that son of a bitch burn right alongside my father. But no. The fella with Kurt today matched his other goon in size, yet had glossy black hair that waved to the nape of his neck. While he was dressed in a tailored suit, the prison tattoos across his knuckles made it clear this was no mere driver.

Watching from the window of a top floor room, I purposely moved the curtains on either side of me. Let him see that and reconsider joining his boss inside. While I in no way believed him to be a good person—only the soulless could see the type of man my father was and continue to work for him—I held no ill will towards this particular meat sack. Meaning, I had no intentions of harming him... unless he gave me no choice.

Late afternoon shadows stretched long fingers across the overgrown lawn, marking the path where the sun would soon hang its weary head on the passing of another day. How many of them I had spent within Crane's Roost Inn, I could no longer say. When the living were absent from the grounds, I seemed to be absorbed by the inn itself, fading into its woodwork as nothing more than a memory that once was. But when life returned, I emerged alert and ready. Especially in the case of Kurt Crane.

This was the moment I'd planned for.

This would make all I'd sacrificed worthwhile.

If my heart still beat, I had no doubt it would have been hammering against my ribs in fervent anticipation as I watched my father climb out from the plush leather seat of his Caddy. Cane gripped tightly in his gnarled hand, he leaned his weight against it and heaved himself to his feet. Gray slacks. Polished shoes. A pale yellow button-down shirt topped by a black sport coat.

His ensemble made a huff of laughter escape me. "He dressed for his death. How nice."

Shielding his eyes from the sun, Kurt peered up at the inn with visible annoyance. Shoulders tight. Jaw clenched. Nostrils flaring in disgust.

"Don't worry, Daddy. The hotel feels the same way about you."

He muttered something to his driver that looked like *Let's get this over with*, then the pair strode toward the front entrance. It was time. Job one would be getting them separated, then the *real* fun could begin. I merely entertained that gleeful thought before my will whisked me downstairs, allowing me to move between the two men unseen.

"Where is this hippie chick show host?" my father huffed, his gaze searching the foyer of the crumbling structure in open contempt. "She was so damned insistent on me coming here, and yet she had time to—what? Run off to paint her nails and get a coffee?"

His driver bent down to retrieve a broken camera lens left on the floor by Summer's crew when they rushed off. Still in a squat, he stared out the open door with his brows furrowed in question. "There are deep tire ruts outside, and this broken piece of equipment costs over three-hundred dollars, easy. Why does it look like someone ran out of here like the devil was chasing them?"

Kurt jabbed the end of his cane in the driver's direction. "Don't start that shit, Travis. You've listened to too many ghost stories about this place. The most we have to worry about is asbestos and that nit wit, D-list celebrity wasting my damned time. Now get up and help me find her!"

Travis, as I now knew him to be named, rose to his full height wearing the expression of a scolded toddler, his face reddening with embarrassment. "Yes, sir. Where should we check first?"

Stabbing his cane against the cracked Spanish tiles, my father folded his hands over its handle and glared in his cohort's direction as if trying to murder him with his stare—which may have been one of the few ways he *hadn't* actually taken a life. "You want to hold hands and walk together through the big, scary hotel? Or could you grow a pair so we can split up and find this bitch faster?"

"Yes, sir. Of course!" Travis snapped to attention, eager to please. "I could search the downstairs and outside, if you want to take the upper levels?"

My father ground his teeth tightly and gave his cane two sharp raps against the floor to remind his dim-witted aid of his need for it. "Yes, by all means, the man with the cane should be the one to maneuver *the stairs*."

"Right, of course!" Travis acknowledged his own idiocy by smacking himself in the forehead with the palm of his hand hard enough to make me wince. "I'll go upstairs, you stay down." He darted in the direction of the staircase, but paused only three strides in. "Quick question. What should I do if I find something?"

Lips pressed together in a thin white line, my father's gaze drifted skyward for a beat, as if begging heaven for the strength to deal with this moron. His chin then snapped in the driver's direction, flames of fury burning behind his eyes. "Bring her to me!" he roared at an octave that made Travis scurry away with his tail tucked.

It was nice of them to separate themselves for me.

It would make what I had to do *so* much easier.

I moved around Travis as little more than a soft breeze, cocooning him with the energy of my essence. My voice, whispered against his ear, planted the seed of my intentions. "Up the stairs, first door on the right."

I trailed behind him as he took the stairs of the grand staircase two at a time, completely obliviously to how they creaked and moaned in protest under his weight. The second floor was dark, lit only by the fading daylight that filtered in from the windows in the domed ceiling of the lobby.

A stronger-willed individual may have hesitated at the top of the stairs, giving pause as they deliberated over where they wanted to go and what they had been told to do. But this was a man used to taking orders. Travis immediately swiveled to the right and barged through the first door he found.

It was a simple trick, really; the first I learned to master after absorbing the energy of the Algea—manipulating the inn as I needed it. No sooner did he charge through that door, than he found himself spilled back out in the driveway. Brow creased, he pulled back in confusion, evaluated his surroundings, and darted back inside. This time, the front door deposited him back at the top of the staircase, where he instinctively chose that same door... and tumbled right back outside. How long that loop would keep him busy, I couldn't say. But, judging by the zest he put into the task, I believed I'd bought myself a good chunk of time.

Now... to locate my father.

A shudder rippled through me as I returned to corporeal form.

Considering I hadn't eaten or slept since I arrived, I imagined I looked a fright.

Good.

This wasn't a moment for vanity. When the time came, I wanted him to see me. To face his sins and admit to being the monster he was. For that to happen, I had to ensure escape wasn't an option. My desire bolted all the windows. The doors locked at my will. (Except for the faux door with which Travis continued to battle.) Nature itself seemed to sense the trouble brewing and responded as heavy storm clouds rolled in, robbing the inn of what little light it possessed. Lightning cracked in time with my growing anger, which ignited every pillar candle positioned throughout the inn. Their flames clawed and stretched for the ceiling in giddy delight for what was to come. Doors opened and slammed shut in the first-floor rooms, signaling me to where my father had wandered.

I heard him before I saw him, his heavy footfalls echoing down the hall. Exiting room twelve and crossing to the door marked thirteen, my father called out to his associate. "Travis? Do you see anything? I have no idea where this prissy bitch got off to. She insisted I come here. If she wasted my time, so help me..."

Using a master key, my father clicked open the lock to room thirteen and disappeared inside. Raising two fingers beside my face, I snapped my wrist in a half-circle motion. The door slammed shut behind him and locked.

"Travis? What the hell are you doing? I'm not playing games!" Kurt Crane's muffled shouts resonated through the six-panel door, making a devilish grin curl across my features.

Calling a pillar candle to my waiting palm, I watched for a moment as its golden light played off my blackened fingertips. "Nor am I, Father. Not anymore."

Casting that ominous promise out to the world, I let the candle roll from my hand and tumble down to the rug runner that ran the length of the hall. The dusty, aged fabric acted as kindling that quickly ignited, sizzling and crackling as the flames grew.

With a wall of fiery death growing and stretching behind me, I stood before room thirteen and allowed the door to slowly creak open. My father spun, a gasp escaping his parted lips as his eyes bulged at the sight of the licking flames.

"Miss Reiz, is that you?" Kurt's eyes narrowed, trying to make sense of what he was seeing. "What's the meaning of this? What have you done? That's malicious destruction of property, young lady, and I will not stand for it! We need to get out of here at once, then we will discuss this!"

"The only place you're going is to hell." Voice an inhuman rasp, I let the flames reveal me. By my iron will alone, I allowed him to see me as I was in life... at first. Long dark hair. Unmarred skin. A young woman with a lifetime of opportunities before her... soon to be snuffed out.

His sharp intake of air thrilled me. "Mallory?"

"It's Malaria now." I took one step closer, then another.

As I inched forward, I allowed a touch more decay to show through.

Skin dulling to a bloodless gray.

Eyes and cheeks sinking in.

Irises blinking to lifeless white orbs.

Lips cracking.

Teeth black.

Every bit the rotting worm fodder he made me.

With no more than an arm's distance between us, I tilted my head and peered up at him, allowing him to take in the horrific spectacle I had become. "You know, like the disease that wriggles into the veins of its victims and kills them from the inside out."

My father stumbled back a step. "What kind of sick joke is this? Who are you? Who put you up to this?" His gaze kept flicking from my face to the raging blaze behind me.

"It's me, Daddy. I just wanted to see you." I pressed further into the room, a gruesome smile tugging at the corners of my decaying lips. "To show you... what you did to me."

His head shook slowly at first, gaining speed and urgency with each flick of his jowled chin. "No! I never harmed you. I would never—"

"No, I suppose *you* wouldn't." My ominous chuckle echoed off the hotel room walls, melding with the cracks and hisses of the flames. "Because you don't like to get your hands dirty. But you *did* order Dex to kill me, just like you ordered Gizmo to be poisoned. Did you think you could escape judgment forever? That your sins would go unpunished?"

My father's nostrils flared, his face reddening with rage. "What do you want from me?"

"What do I want?" The words left my blackened lips in a chilling rasp. "To watch you burn, of course."

Bolting past me, he ran for the door, only to be stopped by a fresh wave of flames bursting through the open door.

Slowly, I turned to face him. "Tell me; what is it you think you have to live for? You've killed everyone who ever cared for you."

In four wide strides, my father made it from the door to the window. Curling his fingers around one of the one-by-sixes boarding it up, he gritted his teeth and tried to pry it free with his bare hands. "You'd be surprised how many people flock to you when you have money," he snapped. "I have no shortage of people who care for me. And, at the risk of sounding redundant.." A sliver of wood took a chunk out of his finger. As drops of blood bloomed from the wound, Kurt paused and popped the digit in his mouth to clean it. "*I have never hurt anyone*!"

The temperature of the room rose to sweltering proportions as flames crept into the room and stretched towards the ceiling. "I'll be able to say the same, even after I watch your carcass burn. Because it will act as the executioner doing my bidding, as Dex did for you. You're a monster, Father, and now your sins have caught up with you."

"And yet you're moments from becoming just like him." Finnick walked through the wall shared with the room to the left of us.

Nostrils flaring, I made no attempts to hide my annoyance— which was a terrifying look for a corpse. "I thought I made it clear I didn't want you here. Are you really that obtuse at taking a hint?"

"Please help me! She's trying to kill me!" Sprinting to Finnick, Kurt tried to grab at his coat, only to have his hands pass right through him. "What is this? Who are you?"

"Don't you recognize me?" Finnick glared at my father, the ruthless rage etched across his handsome features giving me a naughty little thrill. "You ordered your lackey to inject poison into my veins, then had me tossed into a freezer to die. I cannot stress strongly enough that *I'm not here for you.*"

Tendons in my neck snapped and popped as I tilted my head. "You, of all people, should know I don't need saving."

Something that resembled sorrow creased Finnick's brow. "I'm very sorry, Malaria, but this isn't about you, either. It's about her..." Trailing off, he pointed to the corner of the room, between the vanity table and the outside wall.

Had it not been for the glow of the flames, I wouldn't have seen her. Yet there, hunkered in the corner with her hands white knuckling the edge of the vanity, sat Summer. Her eyes were saucers. Her chin trembled. Tear tracks sliced through the grime that covered her ashen face.

And that... was all my doing.

"Yes! The girl! There's a girl here!" The despicable Mr. Crane dashed to her side as fast as he and his cane could hobble and tried to hoist her from the floor with one arm. "Please, help me get her out of here!"

I shook my head, unwilling to accept this as truth. *No, this wasn't right. This wasn't part of the plan!* "What is she doing here? Her crew cleared out days ago!"

Rolling his eyes at my father's obvious attempt to gain sympathy, Finnick walked right through him to get closer to me. "That's what I was trying to tell you before you activated the ring and booted me across the Veil. You touched her heart with your essence and never fully severed that tie. She's been roaming these halls, lost, ever since. Her crew thought she left. That's why they packed up and went in search of her. Sadly, they left her behind, trapped and unable to escape."

I clamped my hands over my mouth, a hot rush of black tears welling behind my lashes. "I never meant to hurt her. I just wanted to get my father here."

Kurt returned to his task of prying the boards off the window. "It sounds like you have a bit more of your father's nature in you than you thought. We may not like it, but people get hurt when they stand in the way of our ambition." With the side of his knee, he bumped Summer's leg. "You, there – help me loosen these boards and we can climb to freedom."

If she heard him, Summer didn't let on. She sat frozen in a catatonic state.

My father's words stabbed into my heart, grinding deep. "I am *nothing* like you!"

Finnick caught hold of my upper arms and swiveled me away from Kurt Crane's blatant toxicity. "You're right. You're nothing like him. You haven't hurt innocent people to further your own agenda... *yet*. But those flames are creeping closer. If you allow Summer to be consumed by them, you will be repeating his pattern. Don't let that happen. Don't let him win. Before it's too late, please put a stop to this."

Peering up at his beautiful face, a bit of the anguish of watching him die seeped in, shattering my long-stilled heart once more. "That's not true. Someone *was* hurt. *You*. You never would have been at his office if it wasn't for me. I made a mistake and you paid with your life."

Finnick took my darkened hands in both of his and dotted kisses to my knuckles. "You had no way of knowing what would happen. The blame lies with him, not you. As a parent, he was meant to build you up. Instead, he created fissures in the foundation of your being. But, here's the thing. Just because you have cracks doesn't mean you're broken. Mistakes of the past will never define you... unless you allow them to. Don't grant them that power. Strive to do better, to be better, and break the pattern of that which haunts you."

My mouth fell open, inky black tears streaking my face as I watched the crackling flames catch the rug and inch closer. "I... don't know how to stop it," I admitted in little more than a whisper.

A beam cracked overhead, raining smoldering embers down on us all.

With one arm shielding his head, Finnick drew me closer with a protective hand on the small of my back. "About that... I think I have an idea. Altering realities for people in this place; how do you do that?"

Not following where he was going with this, I frantically shook my head. "I... I don't know. It's a trick I picked up from the Algea. I focus on what I want and it happens. I'm probably not explaining this right, but the inferno is rather distracting."

Kurt fell to his knees. Positioning himself between us and Summer, he pressed his hands together in a prayer pose. *"Please! I'm begging you! Get me... I mean us out of here!"*

Finnick gave no indication he heard his pleas. "That's perfect." His fingers laced with mine. "Make it your will, and cast me out."

My grip tightened on his hands. A sizzle cut through the room as the curtains ignited. Beside the vanity table, Summer whimpered and buried her head against her knees.

"I don't know what that will do to you." Panic dripped from each word, slathered on by my instant regret. "What if it rips your essence apart?"

Raising one of my hands to his face, Finnick gently pressed his cheek to my palm. "It will be worth it to prove to you that you're nothing like him. He would never put the needs of others over his own desires. Make the sacrifice needed to cement the fact that you're the better person."

The beam above our heads cracked further, flames chewing away at its insides.

"What will that do?" I yelled to be heard over the roar of the blaze.

Instead of screaming, Finnick pulled me in close and spoke the words against my ear. "In death, I was frozen. Let me go corporeal and cast out my essence. Let me use my chill to extinguish the fire. We have no other choice. I won't lose you to this guilt. I trust you and I believe in you, Malaria. Now, it's time to trust in yourself." Sliding off the green aventurine ring, he placed it in my hand. "Finish this. Then, go home."

I may have hesitated.

Insisted we find another way.

Had my father not risen to his feet with his face red and hands curled into indignant fists at his sides. "I did what I had to in order to protect my legacy! I will *never* apologize for that!"

I let my gaze fall in Kurt's direction, resignation weighing heavily on my heart. "*I* was your legacy, Daddy. In the end, there was no one to protect me from *you*."

Before my father could form some further pathetic argument, I rose up on tiptoe and treated myself to the soft caress of Finnick's kiss. One moment of tenderness I prayed wouldn't be our last. Then, with my hand still laced with his, I closed my eyes. I focused on the cold chill of his skin. Studied the energy moving between us. I followed the pull of his spirit through his veins to the very core of his being. There, I channeled the strength of the Algea and gave a gentle pulse of my essence. All Finnick had once been exploded in a sudden bomb of icy mist.

Frost covered every surface.

The fire hissed in protest as it extinguished to steam and the temperature of the room dropped to a mid-winter chill.

Worst yet, I couldn't feel any traces of Finnick's presence.

Not anymore.

Nothing but a cold void remained.

Refusing to allow myself to break down over what that could mean, I skirted around my father to where Summer was hiding. I was a ghoulish mess, I knew that. But I didn't have the physical or emotional strength to manage any kind of illusion. Squatting down beside her, I offered her my hand. "I'm sorry for what I did to you. I used you as a pawn, and that wasn't right or fair. If you'll allow me, I'd like to correct that mistake and get you out of here."

Still dutifully bound to me, Summer put her hand in mine without hesitation.

After helping her to her feet, I asked permission to place my hand over her heart. "May I?"

The most she could muster was a nod.

With a delicate touch, I extracted the darkness I'd marked her with and prayed it wouldn't leave a scar.

In a blink, that haunted look vanished from her features and light returned behind her eyes. Her chin trembled with what I hoped was gratitude but guessed to be more related to my nightmarish appearance. "Thank you," she rasped, her voice hoarse from exhaustion and dehydration.

"Let's get you out of here." One arm hovering protectively behind her to steady her, I guided her towards the door.

"That's it?" My father chuckled, stamping his cane against the floor. "From beyond the grave and all you went through to get me here, now you're just going to walk away? It's a good thing you're dead, because you're an utter disappointment. No child of mine would take the weak way out so easily. You're a *disgrace*!"

Summer's steps faltered. Glancing my way, her pretty features crumbled with fear and a trace of pity.

Keeping my expression neutral, I cast one last look at my father.

In that exact instant, the ceiling beam broke free. Attached only by the electric wires fed through it, it swung down in a wide arc and crunched Kurt Crane's skull against the wall behind him. The gruesome sound it made was a hollow squish no living being could have survived.

My influence didn't free that board, but I won't lie and say I was troubled by the path of its trajectory.

Noting how Summer's complexion morphed from a lovely olive shade to sickly green, I took a step back to clear the path to the front door. "Feel free to run out of here screaming."

She needed no further encouragement. Her footfalls hammered down the hall, followed by the unmistakable sound of the front door being thrown open.

"Mallory?"

Not the least bit surprised, I turned back towards the sound of my father's voice.

His ghostly presence stood beside his body, trying to piece together what was happening. "Is this some kind of joke? What is this? What does it mean?"

Clucking my tongue against the roof of my mouth, I shook my head. "Oh, Kurt. You messed up lingering here. You really should have taken that downward escalator to judgment."

He tried to seize hold of his fallen cane, only to have his hand pass through. "How is this possible? What did you do to me?"

"I didn't do this. *You did.* And now, every spirit here knows you've arrived, and they're well aware of the type of man you are." Even as I uttered the words, ghostly figures manifested through the walls.

Timothy.

Clara.

The mother who shared her story with me to reveal the truth.

I thought they had moved on, but no. They were lying in wait for Kurt Crane, and now... they swarmed him. Moving in an inhuman blur of speed, the apparitions ripped his essence apart with their hands and teeth. His panicked shrieks morphed into screams of agony. In seconds, his spirit was reduced to black tendrils that dissipated into nothingness, like they had never been there at all. With his lifeless body still pinned against the wall, the ghostly family took one another's hand and vanished in a brilliant flash of light. Their retribution complete, they moved on to their eternal beyond.

There were still ghosts in Crane's Roost.

There probably always would be.

But today, one of the many veins of darkness injecting this property had finally been rooted out.

Chapter Elven

From what I gathered, Summer ran to the diner down the road to call for help. I released Travis from the loop I'd bound him to, then faded into the shadows as he scoured the hotel for my father and stumbled onto his remains. Shortly after that, the property buzzed with activity. Cops roped off the scene. The medical examiner pulled up in his black van to collect the body. A Lincoln Town car delivered the Crane Enterprise Board of Trustees to the scene to answer what questions they could about my father's business dealings.

"We've been wanting to tear this place down for years. He simply wouldn't hear of it."

"This hotel should be burned to the ground and the earth salted."

"I have no idea why he would come here. He's retired; all decisions go through us."

"Wait... he owns a property in Florida?"

Kurt Crane left more questions than answers behind as his laundry list of sins came to light. His facility in Florida was stormed by a SWAT team. It was soon discovered that many of the patients there were admitted by their families and held in drug-induced stupors against their will. My father may have gone down, but he took a hell of a lot of people with him. His precise recordkeeping pointed directly to those who paid him to keep his *patients* shackled and quiet.

I watched all of this play out... then things died down and the inn grew quiet once more.

Fresh news stories wiped the thoughts of Crane's Roost from mainstream media. It returned to being a tomb that adventure seekers snuck into for the thrill of, hopefully, coming face-to-face with the grisly darkness that tainted this land and soaked the earth with blood.

My work was done.

Kurt Crane had faced his eternal judgment.

Yet there I lingered, wandering those long halls alongside the other lost souls. Not by choice, mind you. I ached for Carnage Crossing. I had even slid the green aventurine ring on my finger, my hand trembling with longing to give it the half-turn needed to cast me back across the Veil. Still... I stayed.

Wishing Finnick would return.

Praying to see some trace of him.

As the days stretched on, hope dwindled and died.

I saw no other answer.

I'd exorcised him with my will alone.

He sacrificed himself to save me from the darkness hellbent on consuming me.

Just like with Gizmo, I never got to say a proper goodbye. Now, minutes, hours, and days ticked by with me simply existing. My thoughts lingered on the fragmented memories that took me down this path. So often we say *If I knew then what I know now,* as if the knowledge we gained was power. That wasn't the case for me. Those holes in my memories were meant to protect me. To shield me from truths I wasn't prepared to deal with and betrayals no one should have to endure. In the end, the cost for chasing those answers was far too steep... and I paid it in full.

How could I return to Carnage Crossing and pretend everything was just as it had been when it never would be again?

That was why I slid off the ring and tucked it in a drawer of the vanity table my father had died beside. Removing temptation to return home, I accepted my fate as yet another lost soul. One more haunt in this tragic piece of real estate. Unlike the others, I didn't have a death scene to endure day after day. Instead, I gave myself an equally painful pastime. A self-induced loop, like the one I'd trapped Travis in, allowed me to play through my last moments with Finnick. I would close my eyes and hear his voice. Hold out my hand and pray with every ounce of my being that I would feel his fingers link with mine.

"You're right. You're nothing like him."

"Just because you have cracks doesn't mean you're broken."

"I trust you and I believe in you, Malaria."

"Break the pattern of that which haunts you."

Oh, how I wished I could.

How much time passed, I couldn't say. A harsh winter came and went. Buds began to form on the trees outside. With the morning sun came the sweet songs of birds ready to greet another day. Their trilled chirps barely registered through the fog of despair in which I'd been lost. What did break through was the roar of a wrecking ball and a bulldozer crunching over the gravel outside. Machinery beeped and whirred. Crews busied themselves angling equipment into the proper positions. People in hard hats screamed at each other over the noise.

"The boss says we level it."

"Seems a shame. It's a beautiful place."

"Read a bit of history. You couldn't pay me enough to step inside."

All the time I had spent there. The weeks I wasted. Yet it was the thought of being stuck wandering an empty field forever that spurred me into action. This girl doesn't camp. As the wrecking ball connected with the front wall of the grand foyer, I sprinted for the drawer where I'd stashed my ring. The ground trembled beneath my feet, the walls crumbling around me. Soon my family's legacy would be little more than rubble. Once the ring was securely in my hand, I made my escape with little more than a thought.

Outside on the lawn, hidden from the eyes of the living, I watched as Crane's Roost Inn was leveled. Staircase reduced to kindling. Fountain ripped from its base. Bar obliterated with one swing of the wrecking ball.

"You planning to put that ring on now?" Tempest's tone was conversational as she sauntered up beside me.

Letting my gaze sweep over her, I rolled my eyes. "What in Legba's name are you wearing?"

Hands in the pockets of her high collared ensemble, she glanced down with a slight smile playing over her lips. "What? It's a black romper. You haven't been in Carnage Crossing to dress me, so I had Sparrow sew something that would be comfortable and fashionable. It buttons down, with the kind of crisp collar you love."

"The fact that it burns easy is literally the only plus to that entire debacle," I scoffed, my stare traveling back to the destruction before us.

Tempest bumped my elbow with hers. "Normally, I hold your fashion sense in the highest regard. However, and I mean this in the kindest way possible, you look like a ghoul who's been living in a haunted hotel without food or sleep for months on end. What is this you're wearing? Rags strategically placed to prevent the ta-tas and cooter from popping out?"

"It was a peasant blouse and leggings, once upon a time." Even I heard the wistful tone that crept into my voice as I watched the front loader dig out a chunk of the inground pool.

The Queen followed my stare, her chin raised out of the habit of supporting her crown. "That's what happens when things are left alone too long. Time grinds its heel into them as it marches on."

I dragged my tongue over my top teeth and shot her a side-eye glare. "Is that supposed to be some sort of dig at me?"

Her stare pointedly locked with mine. "It absolutely was. And not a subtle one at that. You did what you came here to do, Malaria. You got the answers to your fragmented memories. Deep down, you must have realized there was a risk that what you uncovered would be ugly and unpleasant."

I snorted a humorless huff of laughter. "My father ordered me to be killed. That goes beyond unpleasant. Some might even say it bypassed rude and went straight to traumatizing."

"It's horrific. I completely agree." Swiveling on the balls of her feet, the Queen planted herself in a firm stance to face me. "Is your plan to let it break you?"

I jerked as if she'd slapped me. "Of course not, but a little time to heal is allowed."

"This has not been healing." Tempest waved her arm in the direction of the wreckage of the inn. "*This* has been wallowing. You shut everyone out and stayed here alone, trapped with your own dark thoughts. I know it sucks to ask for help. I get that what happened here broke your heart in ways you never imagined possible. But when you close yourself off and let your thoughts spiral, those wounds can't heal. All they can do is fester."

Jaw clenched tight, I fought back a wave of emotion brought on by the truth in her words. Tears stung behind my eyes, yet I refused to shed them in front of her. After all, I had a reputation to protect. "How do I go back and pretend I didn't have my cold, lifeless heart ripped from my chest and stomped into the dirt?"

"You don't." Tempest shrugged, her features softening. "You surround yourself with the people who care about you and keep trudging through this afterlife until the pain lessens and the scars heal."

My fingers tightened around the ring in my hand, the longing for home making it heat against my skin. "You're maddeningly optimistic. Do you know that about yourself?"

A smile warming her face, the Queen joined me once more in watching what remained of my family legacy being pulverized. "I could always try *your* methods, where I use abrasive behavior and barely concealed threats as a means of motivation."

"Say what you want, but it works."

We shared a chuckle, then silence fell.

Me wrestling with a million different intrusive thoughts, and her giving me a moment to weigh them for merit. Only one seemed important enough to give voice to. "I cast Finnick out and he disappeared in a spray of frost. What if he comes back here? Fights his way back to me only to find me gone? I can't abandon him like that after all he sacrificed."

"Oh, I forgot to mention that." Tempest fought back a cat who ate the canary grin. "Finnick is back in Carnage Crossing, although he prefers to go by Finn now. I'm afraid his last visit with you left him rather worn out and his recovery rendered him unable to make it back across the Veil. Not for lack of trying, I can assure you. Persistent thing that he is, he's been hounding me to come and find you. I had thought giving you space to work things out would bring you back of your own volition. Clearly, I underestimated how stubborn you are. Not that I'm the least bit surprised."

I blinked her way. Once. Twice. And again. "Finnick… Finn… is back in Carnage Crossing and you didn't lead with that?"

Head tilted, she tipped her chin my way. "You're Malaria Cain. I thought it would take more than *a man* to persuade a badass like you."

I was nodding my agreement when the hotel's tower suite smashed to the ground, kicking up a huge dust cloud. "You're absolutely right. Had you started with that, I would have said it was good he's a safe distance away from me. What about Carnage Crossing? Is it still in a state of chaotic mess?"

Tempest wet her lips and shook her head. "No, when your father died, everything calmed down and returned to normal. The turmoil you were feeling from this side of the Veil was infecting us all. That's how powerfully your presence is felt by our people. We never closed the Veil, Malaria. We never shut you out. We weathered the storm alongside you, in hopes you would return home. Your father is gone. The Crane's Roost Inn is demolished. So, you tell me, what do you want to do?"

Squaring my shoulders, I slid the ring on, instantly feeling the jolt of energy coursing through it. "I want... to finally let this portion of my existence rest in peace."

Chapter Twelve

If you thought I was the kind of ghoul who immediately ran to find the guy she was interested in as soon as she crossed back over the Veil, you haven't been paying attention. There was someone else I had to connect with first.

Me.

Tempest asked Sparrow to prepare a bath for me at Legba Manor while Bones ventured to my shop to retrieve fresh clothing. After being forced to eat and hydrate, I let myself sink into the blissfully warm tub to scrub away the grime. Once I was thoroughly cleaned, I leaned back in the water and watched the enchanting green and purple lights playing across the skyline. Somewhere in the midst of it, I dozed off for a long overdue nap.

When the water grew cool, I climbed out and toweled off. The dress Bones chose for me was a favorite from my collection. Shimmying into it made me feel more like myself than I'd felt in months. The luxurious fabric was the shade of raven feathers, trimmed in gold. Its sweetheart neckline plunged deep into my cleavage, putting all my glorious scars on full display. The bodice cinched tight at my waist, then cascaded out in a full skirt of flowing layers. Piling my hair on top of my head, I gazed at my reflection as I dotted a bit of lavender oil behind my ears. My skin still had a greyish hue to it and my cheekbones were far more defined than usual. But beyond that, I could see my true face again. The Dark Lady was gone, buried under the rubble of Crane's Roost Inn.

After lacing on a pair of Victorian-inspired boots, I ventured out onto the cobblestone streets. Heels clicking against the stone, I passed Ember as she attempted to coax her owl down from atop her Hollow's End Apothecary sign.

I waved to Enyo, who had the door of Wake the Dead Coffee open to tempt folks inside with the scent of her freshly baked treats.

My own storefront—Death Shroud Clothing & More—called to me, beckoning me to step inside and create.

Not yet.

There would be time for that soon enough.

First, I needed to confirm something to myself. I found my answer in Mortality Estates. When the Crane's Roost Inn was destroyed in the land of the living, it ceased to exist in Carnage Crossing. Where the hotel once stood, now stretched an empty lot of nothingness.

"You could always get a room at the Dead End Resort and Day Spa. I crashed there for a few nights when I first arrived. Other than that creepy little girl with the teddy bear who wanders the halls, it's actually quite a nice place." Hands clasped behind his back, Finn edged up beside me wearing a dapper white suit.

"I have a cot set up at the back of my shop. I'll stay there." I couldn't have fought back that smile if I tried. "Oh, and don't let that little girl disguise fool you. She's more than a hundred years old and takes great pleasure in creeping out the newbies."

"Thanks for the tip." Finn's silver eyes crinkled at the corners, his gaze sweeping the length of me. "It's good to see you. And I mean that quite literally. It's good to see *you*."

"I got lost for a little while. Thank you for reminding me who I am." Locking stares, a million unspoken sentiments hung in the air between us.

Clearing his throat, Finn kicked a stone away with the toe of his shoe. "Since my mother's shop was the last place I was living, it crossed over as my home. Considering there's absolutely no use for a medium here, if you'd ever like a place a smidge larger to stay, you're more than welcome."

My eyebrows lifted to my hairline. "The place where the Queen died is *here*?"

One corner of his mouth tugging back in a half-grin, Finn plunged his hands in the pockets of his crisp white pants. "It sure is.

I was worried it would bother her, but she actually seems to like it. She says it's the spot where her authentic life began."

My thoughts drifted back to the first time I walked into his shop. He was dressed in a sapphire dinner jacket and fiddling with his wooden dice. When he glanced up at me from under his lashes, a part of me I never knew existed awoke. "I completely understand where she's coming from."

Picking up on my not-so-hidden subtext, Finn closed the distance between us. Tracing the knuckle of his index finger along my jawline, he gently guided my face to his. "I need you to know I don't regret one minute of what we went through, because it led me to you."

His lips met mine, the chill of them jolting through me like an electric spark. "I never meant to get you killed," I murmured against his mouth. "But you'll have to pardon me if I can't manage to feel guilty about it at this particular moment."

To my great regret, Finn pulled away. Thankfully, only far enough to place his forehead to mine. "I know you didn't. Did you at least find what you were looking for?"

Blinking up at him, I peered at the ethereal beauty of his icy appearance and felt my long-dead heart warm. "I did. Though I can't say I'm surprised by the answer."

"And what's that?"

"That everything I want and need is right here in Carnage Crossing."

"Well, it is *now*." Wiggling his eyebrows mischievously, he offered me his arm. "Seeing as we have eternity, how about if you help me get better acquainted with this place by giving me the Malaria Cain tour, complete with all the gossip? I mean it – I want all the dirt on this gloriously macabre place."

Hooking my arm with his, I chuckled. "Well, the *really* juicy stuff began right around the time a member of the dead fell in love with one of the living."

"Oh, I think I'm going to like this story..."

About the Author

Stacey Rourke is the award-winning author of works that span genres. She lives in Florida with her husband and two beautiful daughters. She loves to travel, has an unhealthy shoe addiction, and considers herself blessed to make a career out of talking to the imaginary people that live in her head.

Connect with her at:

www.staceyrourke.com
Facebook at www.facebook.com/staceyrourkeauthor
Instagram @rourkewrites

Dead Ringer
Dead as a Doornail

The Unfortunate Soul Chronicles
Rise of the Sea Witch
Entombed in Glass
Pursuing Madness

The Archive of the Five
The Apocalypse Five

Death Diggers Handbook Series
Corpse Queen
Rotting Reign
Divine Decay
Monsters & Mayhem
Chaos & Carnage
Hauntings & Havoc

Made in USA - Crawfordsville, IN
54937_9798359088527
11.08.2022 0742